To Ireland, land of my memories
—E. B.

For Uncle ZZ
—Z. P.

❦

Text Copyright © 2010 Eve Bunting
Illustration Copyright © 2010 Zachary Pullen

Sleeping Bear Press™

315 E. Eisenhower Parkway, Ste. 200
Ann Arbor, MI 48108
www.sleepingbearpress.com

© 2010 Sleeping Bear Press is an imprint of Gale, a part of Cengage Learning.

Printed and bound in the United States of America.

10 9 8 7 6 5 4 3

Library of Congress Cataloging-in-Publication Data

Bunting, Eve, 1928-
Finn McCool and the great fish / written by Eve Bunting;
illustrated by Zachary Pullen.
p. cm.
Summary: Irish giant Finn McCool is told that in order to become
wise he must catch and eat the salmon that possesses knowledge, but
Finn finds that he cannot bring himself to kill the miraculous fish.
ISBN 978-1-58536-366-7
1. Finn MacCumhaill, 3rd cent.—Legends. [1. Finn MacCool—Legends.
2. Folklore—Ireland.] I. Pullen, Zachary, ill. II. Title.
PZ8.1.B875Fi 2010
398.2—dc22
[E]
2009036936

Printed by Bang Printing, Brainerd, MN, 3rd Ptg., 01/2011

finn mccool
and the great fish

Eve Bunting

Illustrated by Zachary Pullen

Finn McCool was the biggest giant in all Ireland. He was the greatest warrior ever known, and his strength was remarkable.

He could lift a house and turn it around so it faced the sun, and another way at night so it faced the moon where it rose over the mountains. If the weather was bad and the men of the village were hurrying to bring in their hay before the rain set in, Finn was ready to help them. He'd lift the carts, horses and all, and carry them to shelter.

"He's the best hearted man that ever walked on Ireland's green grass," the people said. "We're blessed at having him live here with us in Drumnahoon." But they were agreed on one thing that was seldom mentioned. Finn wasn't terrible smart.

"He's a bit of a turnip head," they'd whisper sometimes and smile affectionately. "He doesn't know much. But he's a great big man for all that."

One day Finn heard the whisper and knew it to be true.

In the nearby townland lived an old man who was said to know the source of great wisdom. It was said he had promised to reveal it only to the right one. He was a bit of a mystery, staying sometimes in his house, at other times disappearing for weeks on end. Many a man and many a woman had tried to be friends with him, to wheedle the secret of knowledge out of him.

Simon the Baker had brought him fresh baked soda bread, the butter already thick on it. Bertie O'Hanlon brought him a white hen, the best layer in the village, so he could have a fresh egg for his breakfast of a morning. Bridie Mulligan brought him a barrow load of turf she'd cut herself in the bog. "So you can have a warm fire these frosty nights," she purred.

He thanked them all for their kindness,
but he kept his secret to himself.

It was the day after Bridie's visit that Finn came to him.
He couldn't fit in the house so he sat outside, his hands
resting on the roof.

"Old man," he called. "It's Finn McCool, and I've come
to ask if you'd share the secret of wisdom with me."

The old man came out, and Finn got down on his hunkers so they could see each other right.

"I know who you are, and I was waiting for you to come," the old man said.

"I know you're good and kind as well as big. I know you're a great warrior and a friend to Ireland. I know you beat the giant Culcullan and saved Ireland from the Scots. But I need to ask you one question. With all that you have, why do you need wisdom?"

"A man's nothing without it," Finn said. "With wisdom I'll know better how to help my friends. I'll be able to answer their questions where now I can only shake my head. If I was wise, I could speak for Ireland when the need arose."

The old man nodded. "You're a giant now and a good man. But you'll be more with the grace of wisdom added to you. So listen. In the River Boyne there lives a fish, a great salmon, the red of the sky at sunset. In him is the wisdom of the world. Catch him, cook him, and eat him, and that wisdom will be yours."

"Thank you, sir," Finn said.

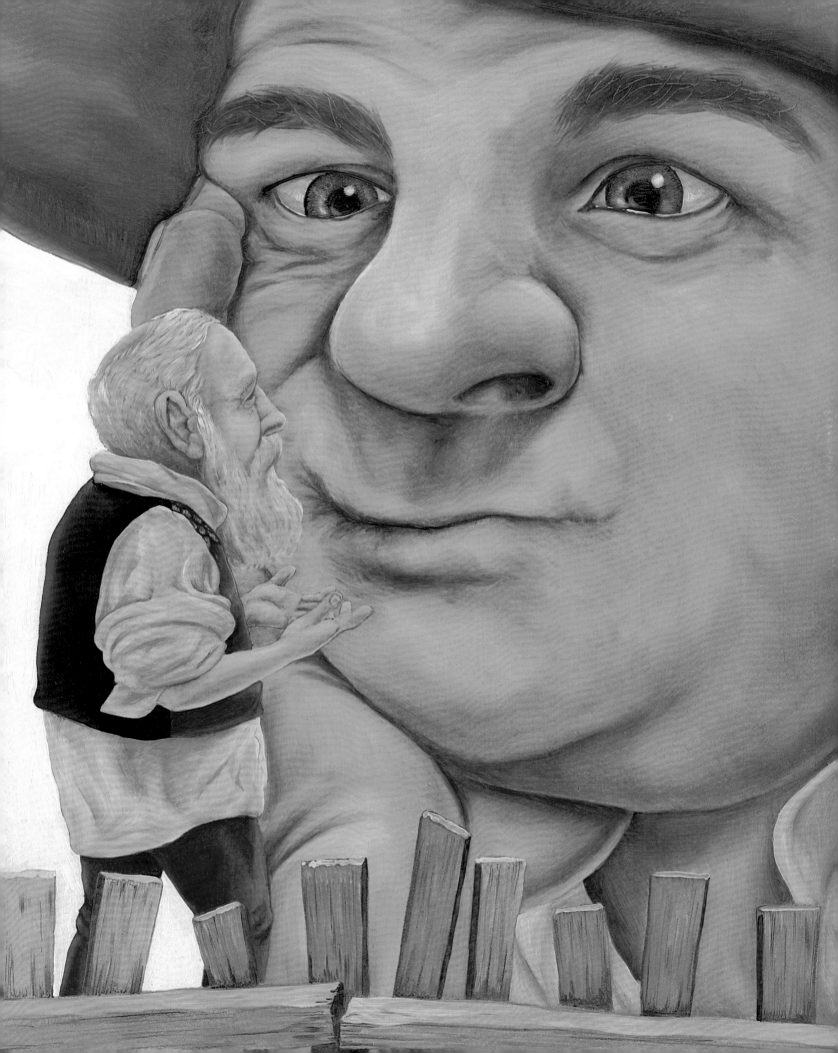

Two strides took him to the River Boyne. He dropped in his line. There were fish in the cool, gurgling waters, brown fish, silver fish, fish with the sheen of a copper penny, but none as red as the sky at sunset.

And then Finn saw the great red salmon swimming lazily upstream. *Gorra*, Finn thought. It's as if it's looking for something. The salmon swam around the line then took the bait and the hook. The River Boyne tossed and tumbled as Finn pulled the fish ashore. There was a mumbling and a rumbling that seemed to come from the river itself, and the idea came to Finn that the river didn't want to let go of its great fish.

"I'm sorry to take it, but I'm after the wisdom," Finn told the river. "A man can make more use of wisdom than a fish can so I ask you to forgive me." He took the fish in his big hand, wondering at the beauty of it. It shimmered and gleamed in the sunlight, every scale a point of fire.

Finn looked in its eyes and saw the wisdom there, all the knowledge of the world. He saw life. How could he kill it? How could he eat it? The thought made him shudder. He spoke to the fish. "You have the wisdom and I wanted it, but not if I have to sacrifice you," he said.

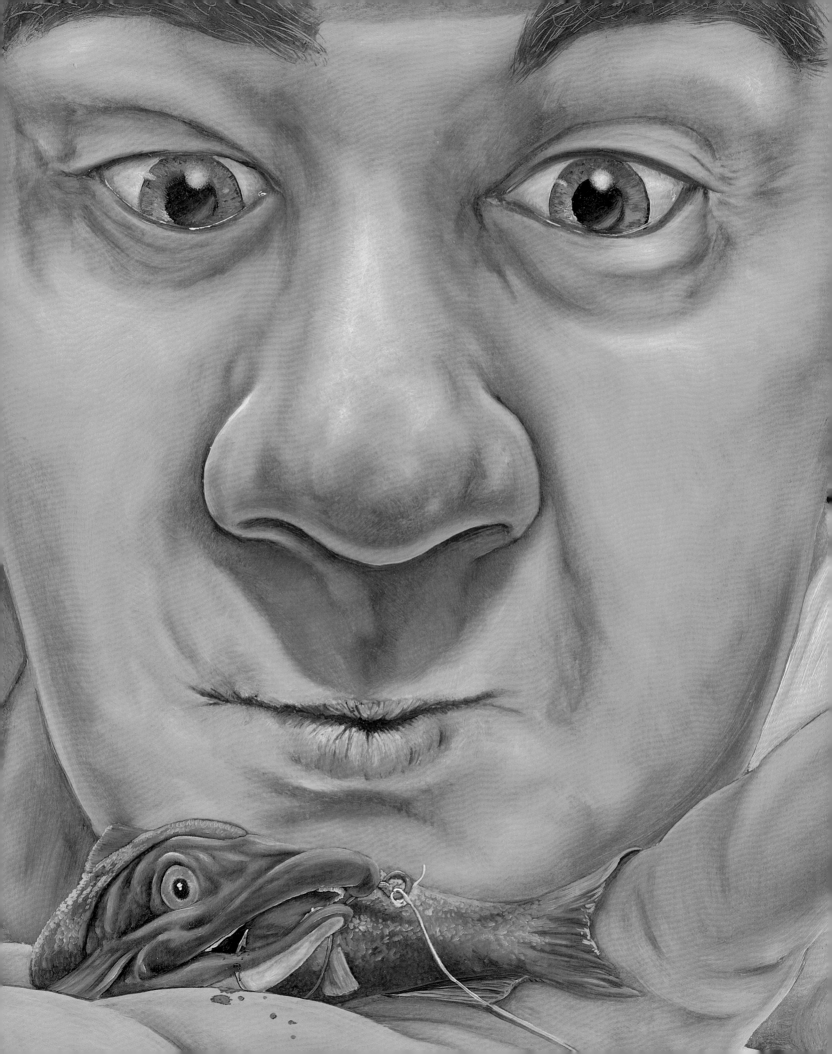

The salmon's lip was bleeding from where the hook had caught in it. "Ach, I'm sorry about that," Finn said, and he carefully eased the shining hook out of the fish's mouth. But it caught in his own thumb and the pain near blinded him. He took his thumb in his mouth and sucked on it and he tasted something he'd never tasted before. His blood, the salmon's blood? There was a tide in him as if something unknown had entered his body, something strange and beautiful.

The fish spoke. "I thank you for sparing my life. I was prepared to let go of it. But now my wisdom has seeped into you along with my blood. It is known to me that you will use it in the service of others and of Ireland."

Finn stared. He'd never heard a fish speak. "But why did you let me catch you, for you are wise enough not to take a baited hook?"

"Maybe I knew whose hook it was. Maybe I've been waiting for you to come."

"Thank you," Finn said. "I will use the gift well."

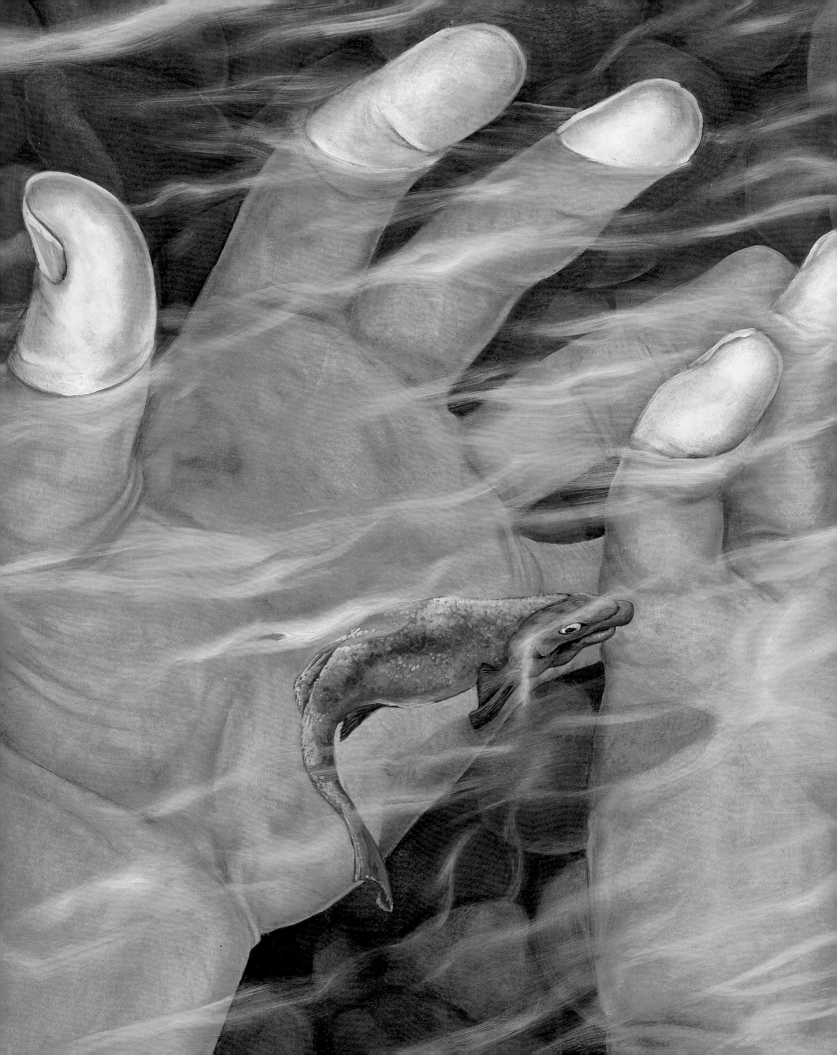

Gently he laid the salmon back in the river
and watched as it swam away. Was it a lighter
shade of red now?

He looked at his thumb. Where the hook had pierced was already healed over, and the thumb itself was turning a delicate shade of pink.

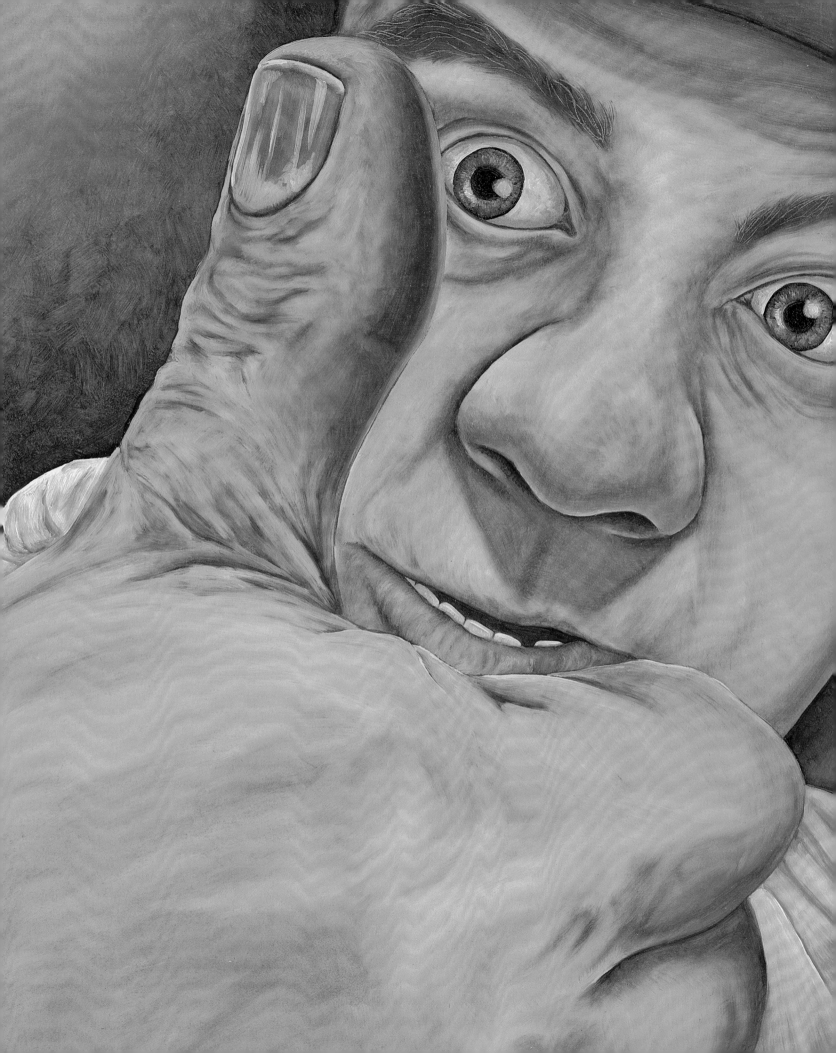

Finn told no one about his encounter with the salmon of wisdom, but he felt a need to tell the old man. He found the house empty, the old man gone. The barrow load of turf sat unused. The soda bread on the kitchen table was uneaten. The eggs in the hen's nest were ungathered.

But on the path was a glittering trail that might have been fish scales, every one a point of fire.

Ever after that the people in the village of Drumnahoon remarked on how wise a man Finn had become, how he'd talked with the King of England and the King of France and presented to them the needs and wants of Ireland.

How he'd saved them from the Viking longships that had crossed the sea to take Irish land. How he knew their own problems and took care of them before they rightly knew them themselves.

"But still, he's the same good Finn he always was," they agreed.

"Isn't it a puzzle, though, the way he sucks his thumb when he's applying his mind to something? You'd almost think there was a magic to it."

You almost would.